# Suho's White Horse
## A MONGOLIAN LEGEND

Retold by Yuzo Otsuka
Illustrated by Suekichi Akaba

Translated by Richard McNamara and Peter Howlett
Instrumental by Li Bo

**R.I.C. Publications**
Dublin • London • Perth • Tokyo

To the north of China is a land called Mongolia. Here lies a great grassland steppe where people have lived as herders, tending their sheep, cattle and horses since long, long ago.

The people in this land play a musical instrument called the *morin khuur* or horse-head fiddle. This two-stringed instrument has a carved horse's head at the top of its neck. But why does it have a horse's head? Here is the story of the origin of this Mongolian fiddle.

On the Mongolian steppes long ago lived a poor shepherd boy named Suho. He lived with his grandmother, just the two of them in their ger*. Suho was young but he was a very hard worker, working the same as any grown man. He'd get up early in the morning to help his grandmother prepare their breakfast and then he would shepherd their twenty-some sheep out on the vast grasslands.

Suho the shepherd also had a beautiful voice. Other shepherds would often ask him to sing. His singing could be heard for miles across the steppes.

*ger   a circular Mongolian felt/canvas tent dwelling

4

One evening, after the sun had set behind the distant hills and darkness had spread over the steppes, the neighbors gathered because Suho, the young shepherd, had still not come home. His grandmother was very worried and everyone was anxious, wondering what had happened to him. When the neighbors were just about to set out to search for him, Suho suddenly appeared, running out of the darkness carrying something white.

Everyone gathered around Suho to see what the white thing was he was carrying. The little white package was a small, newborn foal. Suho beamed with joy as he told the story of how he had found this white foal.

"On my way home, I found this foal. It was struggling to stand. I looked about but I couldn't see its owner or its mother. If I had left it there, I am sure the wolves would have eaten it. So, I brought it home with me."

The days turned into months and Suho raised
the little white colt with all his love and affection.
It grew to be one of the finest yearlings on the
steppes. It had strong features and was as white as
snow. People would often stop and stand looking at
the handsome colt, speechless in admiration.
This colt was Suho's pride and joy.

One night, Suho was awakened by the loud neighing of his colt and the frantic bleating of the sheep. He jumped out of bed and ran to the sheepfold. There in the darkness he could see a giant wolf attacking the sheep. But standing between the wolf and the sheep, fighting off the wolf's attacks, was his little white horse.

Suho chased the wolf off and ran to his brave white colt's side. His body was covered with sweat. He must have been fighting off the wolf for a long time. Rubbing his wet body, Suho spoke quietly to him, just like he would speak to a baby brother.

"My little white horse, you did a great job fighting off that giant wolf. Thank you, my friend – thank you so much."

The years flew by and, one spring, an official challenge was handed down to all the people living on the steppes. The local Governor was to hold a horse race in town and the winner of the race was to be given his daughter's hand in marriage. Suho's shepherd friends urged him to enter the race, saying, "Go on, Suho, ride your white horse and enter the race for us all." Finally, Suho agreed and, sitting high on his beautiful white horse, he rode off to town across the great grasslands to enter the horse race.

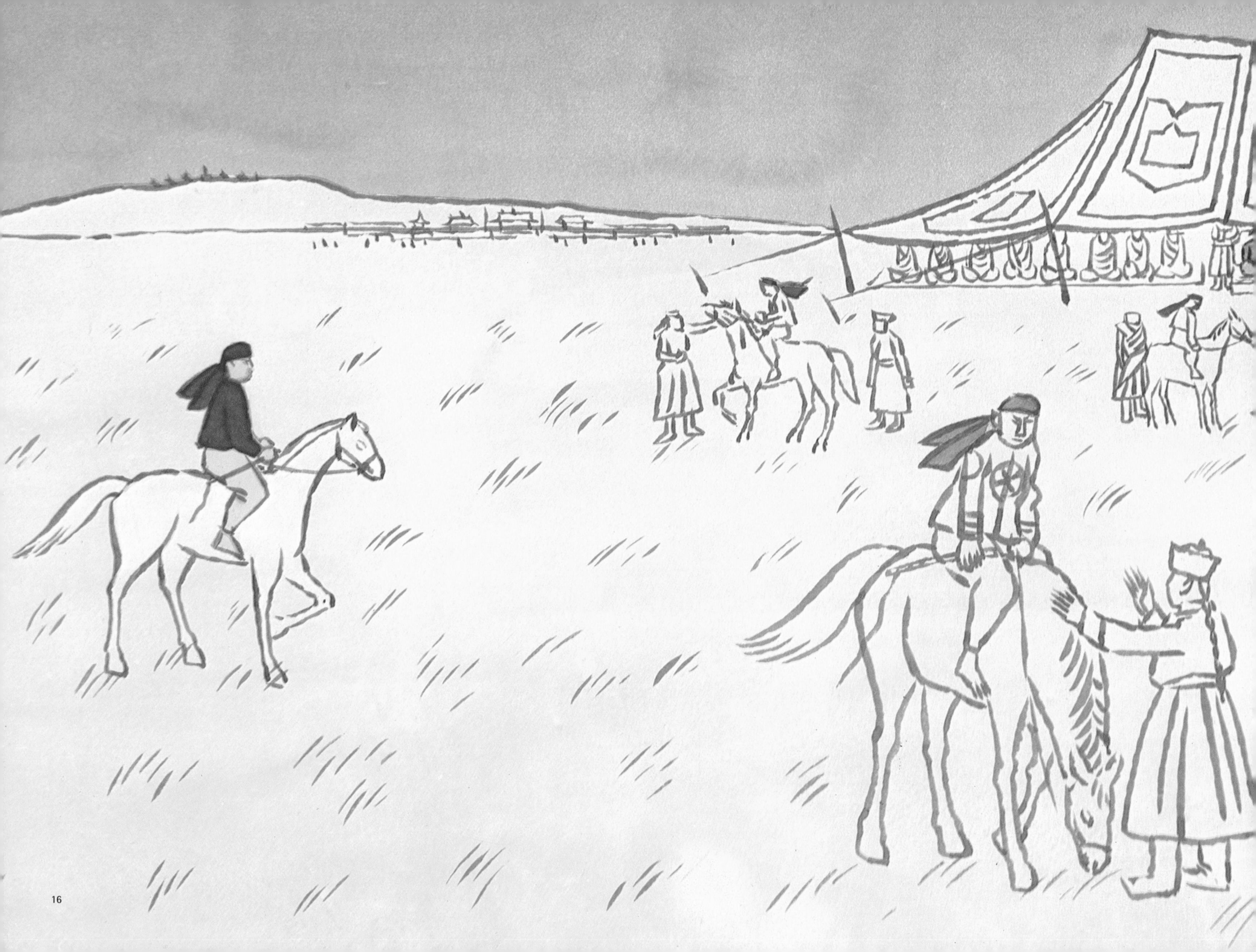

A crowd of spectators had already
gathered at the horse race site.
And there, sitting on a splendid
platform, was the Governor.

The race began and all the finest young riders from throughout the steppes cracked their leather whips – the great race was on!

In a cloud of dust, all the horses charged off across the plains. But far, far ahead, leading them all, was a beautiful white horse with Suho riding on its back.

"The white horse is the winner!" shouted the Governor. "Bring the horse and rider to me at once!"

When the Governor saw that the rider was nothing but a poor shepherd boy, he burst out laughing and refused to give his daughter to Suho. Mockingly, he said, "Here boy, take these three silver coins and be on your way. And as for the white horse, you can leave it right here!"

Suho turned red with anger and shouted, "Governor, I came here to enter a horse race! I didn't come here to sell you my horse!"

"What did you say?" roared the Governor. "How dare you talk to me like that! Guards, beat this fool!"

The guards grabbed Suho. They beat and kicked him until he fell to the ground, unconscious.
Then the Governor, taking the white horse, strutted home, followed by his guards.

Suho was saved by his friend, who carried him all the way home.

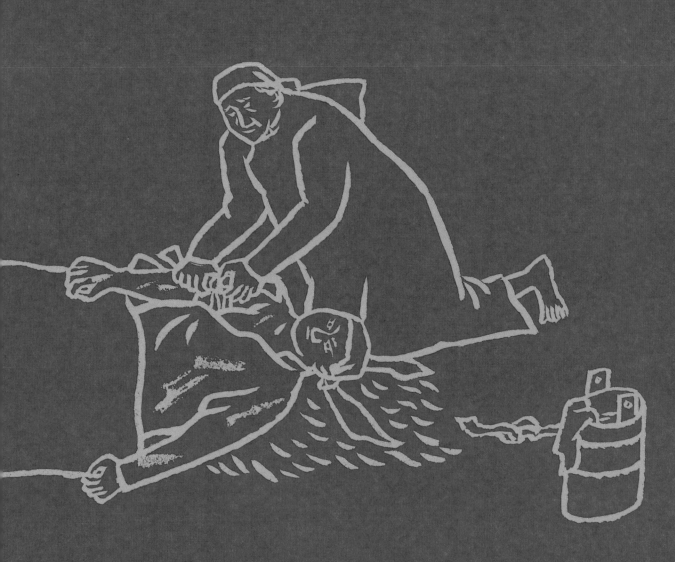

Suho had cuts and bruises all over his body. Grandmother stayed by his side night and day to treat his painful wounds. A week passed and Suho's wounds began to heal. However, Suho's great sorrow at having lost his beloved white horse only grew stronger and stronger.

"I wonder how my horse is?" thought Suho. Thoughts about his white horse filled his mind.

What **had** happened to his white horse?

Meanwhile, across the steppes, the great Governor was very proud of his beautiful horse. In fact, he was so proud that he decided to hold a grand banquet so he could show off his new white horse.

When the banquet was at its height, the great Governor called on his guards to fetch his white horse. He wanted to ride and parade the white horse in front of all his guests.

The Governor climbed up onto the white steed. But just then, the white horse let out a frightening call and kicked up its heels, high into the air, throwing the great Governor from his saddle on to the ground. Then, breaking free, the white horse charged right through the startled guests and galloped off like a gust of wind across the grasslands.

The Governor struggled to his feet and roared, "Guards! Catch my horse! And if you can't catch it, kill it with your arrows!" The guards drew their bows and, all at the same time, released their arrows. The arrows flew through the air with a whistling sound and showered down on the white horse's back. Yet the white horse continued to run.

That night, as Suho was just about falling off to sleep, he heard a strange noise from outside.
"Who is it?" he cried out, but there was no answer. The clattering sound continued, so Grandmother
went outside to see what it was. "Suho, it's the white horse! It's our white horse, Suho!"

Suho jumped out of bed and ran outside. Sure enough, it was his white horse – but he was badly wounded. Many arrows were still embedded in his body. Sweat was pouring from him, for he had run, nonstop, to be with the boy he loved.

Gritting his teeth, Suho began pulling out the arrows, one at a time. Blood gushed out of each wound.

"White horse, oh my beautiful white horse, don't die!" cried Suho.

But the horse grew weaker and weaker. His breathing became shallower and shallower and gradually the light in his eyes faded. By the next morning, Suho's beautiful white horse was dead.

Night after night, Suho lay awake crying. Then, one night when he could cry no more, he fell asleep and had a dream. In his dream he was stroking his white horse. The white horse nuzzled Suho and spoke to him softly, "Don't be so sad, Suho. Take my bones, my hide, my tendons, and my hairs – use them to make a musical instrument. If you do this, I can always be by your side, and I can always comfort you."

As soon as Suho awoke from his dream, he went to work.
Using the bones, hide, tendons and hairs, just as the white horse
had told him to, Suho quickly constructed the musical instrument.

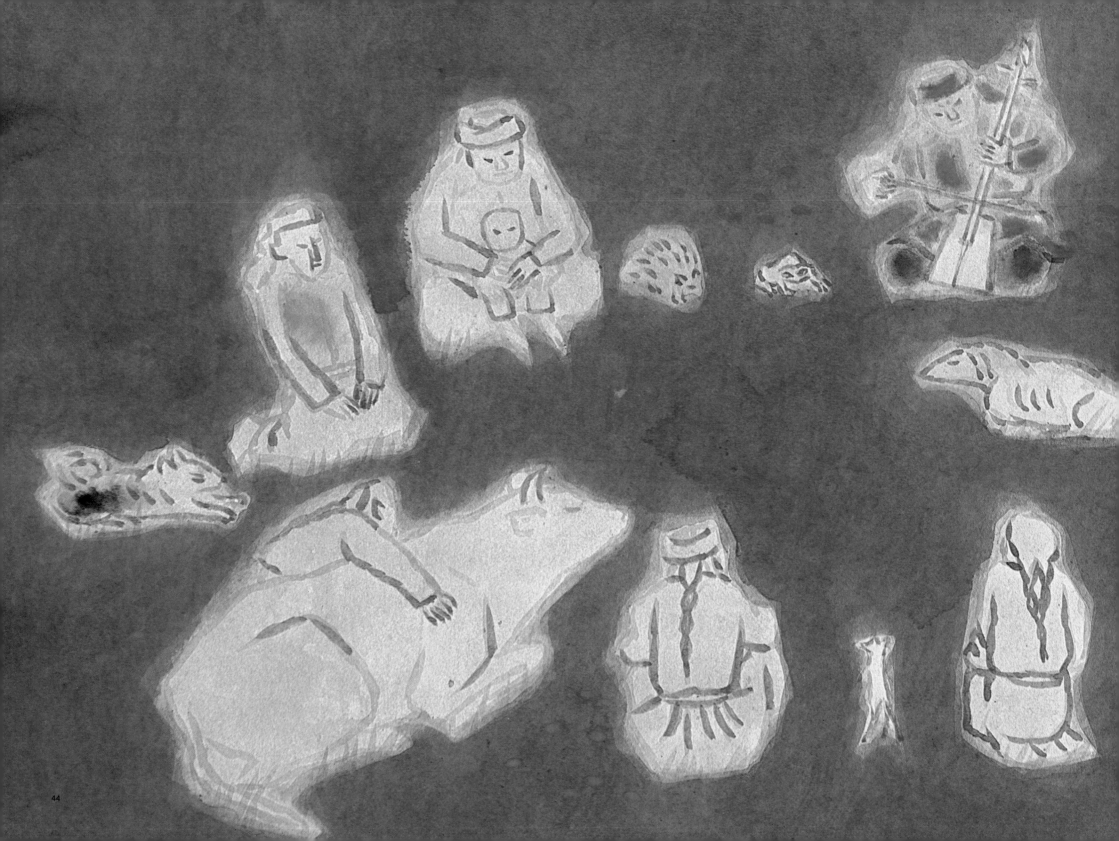

The musical instrument was finished. It was called the *morin khuur*, or horse-head fiddle. Wherever Suho went, he always took this fiddle with him. Every time he played it, he was reminded of how his precious white horse had been killed and feelings of pain welled up inside. But he was also able to remember the happy days spent riding across the wide grasslands, mounted on his white horse. When he played his fiddle it always felt like the white horse was right by his side. At times like these, the sound of the fiddle would resound more beautifully than ever and it moved the hearts of all those who listened to its deep, rich tones.

The years passed and gradually the horse-head fiddle became popular throughout the Mongolian steppes. And so, to this day, when dusk falls over the vast grasslands, the shepherds gather together to listen to the low and gentle sounds of the horse-head fiddle. Its soothing sound helps them to forget all the pains and worries of the day and fills them with peace and new strength.

THE END

## Author

**Yuzo Otsuka**  was born in 1921 in Manchuria, now known as Northeastern China. He graduated from Tokyo University Faculty of Law in 1942. After working for some years in the Editorial Department of Heibonsha Publishing Co. he became involved in the translation and introduction of children's literature from throughout the world. Some of his most popular translations are A. Lindgren's *Pippi Longstockings*, (Iwanami Shoten Publishers), Mark Twain's *The Adventures of Tom Sawyer*, *Hundred and one Grimm Marchen*, *Andersen Fairy Tales* (Fukuinkan Shoten Publishers).  Picture books he has translated and retold include: *Punkhu Maincha, the Story of Dhon Cholecha, The Story of the Stone Lion* – based on a Tibetan tale, *A Big Canoe* (Fukuinkan Shoten Publishers).  He lives in Chiba Prefecture.

## Illustrator

**Suekichi Akaba**  (1910~1990) Born in Tokyo, Akaba was a self-taught artist. In 1932 he travelled to Manchuria (Northeastern China) where he worked in a transportation company and later a telegram and telephone company. During his stay in Manchuria, he exhibited his art in The All Manchuria Art Exhibit and was awarded the highest honors three times. On his return to Japan in 1947 he worked as an art designer and published his first picture book, *Rokujizo and the Hats*, when he was 50. He went on to illustrate numerous books. Some of his best-loved books include, *Momotaro the Peach Boy – An Old Japanese Tale*, *Oniroku and the Carpenter*, *The Crane Wife – A Japanese Folk Tale*, *The Tongue-cut Sparrow* (Fukuinkan Shoten Publishers), *The White Dragon and the Black Dragon* (Iwanami Shoten Publishers).

Akaba received many awards in Japan for his outstanding works: The Sankei Children's Literature and Culture Award, The Kodansha Literature and Culture Award, and The Shogakkan Painting Award are but a few.

After his works were translated into over ten languages, he won international acclaim, being awarded among others The American Brooklyn Museum of Art – Children's Picture Book Award and the most prestigious Hans Christian Andersen Award for Illustration – 1980, often called the Little Nobel Prize. He is one of only two Japanese to ever receive this award. Over 6000 of his original paintings have been donated to the Chihiro Art Museum, Azumino and almost all of his books have been donated to the Fukazawa Library in Kamakura City.

## Morin Khuur Musician

Born in 1955 in the Xilingoro Reigion of Inner Mongolia, **Li Bo** started playing the *morin khuur* when he was ten years old, becoming a professional player when he turned 15.

In 1987 he graduated from the Inner Mongolia University of Education's Department of Music Composition and is now considered to be one of the world's best *morin khuur* players. He has performed with The Chinese National Symphony Orchestra and musicians like the guitarist Atsumasa Nakabayashi, the cellist Ludorit Kanta and the virtuoso shamisen player Yukichi Yamazato. He helped set up the Morin Khuur Fund<http://www.geocities.co.jp/NatureLand/9876/> which helps to promote cultural exchange between Mongolia and Japan.  He has produced over six CDs, his second being titled *The Legend of the Horse-head Fiddle*. He now lives in Nagoya, Japan, with his wife.

CD includes the epic *morin khuur* instrumental, *Suho's White Horse*, played by the horse-head fiddle's finest player – Li Bo.

## Translators

**Peter Howlett** was born and raised in Hokkaido, Japan and currently teaches at Hakodate La Salle Junior and Senior High Schools. He lives near Hakodate and is married with three children.

**Richard McNamara** is a British-trained psychologist and a graduate of Kumanoto Graduate School of Education. He lives in Aso with his wife and family.

Together, Peter and Richard have translated a large number of Japan's classic children's picture books, including the Guri and Gura series. R.I.C. Story Chest titiles they have translated include, *Elephee's Walk*, *Amy and Ken Visit Grandma* and *Groompa's Kindergarten*.

## Suho's White Horse
### A Mongolian Legend

Text © Yuzo Otsuka 1967

Illustrations © Suekichi Akaba 1967

First published by Fukuinkan Shoten Publishers, Inc., Tokyo, Japan.

Re-published under licence by R.I.C. Publications Limited Asia, Tokyo, Japan

Japanese ISBN: 4 902216 17 5
International ISBN: 1 74126 021 3

Printed in Singapore

**Distributed by:**

**Asia**

R.I.C. Publications – Asia
5th Floor, Gotanda Mikado Building,
2-5-8 Hiratsuka, Shinagawa-Ku Tokyo, Japan
142-0051
Tel: (03) 3788 9201
Email: elt@ricpublications.com
Website: www.ricpublications.com

**Australasia**

R.I.C. Publications
PO Box 332
Greenwood
Western Australia 6924
Tel: (618) 9240 9888

**United Kingdom and Ireland**

Prim-Ed Publishing
Bosheen
New Ross
Co. Wexford, Ireland
Tel: (353) 514 40075

**R.I.C.Story Chest**
スーホの白い馬 (英語版)
**Suho's White Horse**
2004年4月30日初版発行

再話 大塚勇三　絵 赤羽末吉
翻訳 ピーター・ハウレット
　　　リチャード・マクナマラ

発行者 ジョン・ムーア
発行所 アールアイシー出版株式会社
　　　〒142-0051
　　　東京都品川区平塚2-5-8
　　　五反田ミカドビル5F
　　　Tel:(03)3788-9201
　　　Fax:(03)3788-9202

ISBN 4-902216-17-5
http://www.ricpublications.com
Printed in Singapore